MARTHA
AND THE
MANGO

DANIEL MORETON

D0607827

SRA
Macmillan/McGraw–Hill
Columbus, Ohio

Copyright © 1993 by Daniel Moreton

Designed by Paul Zakris

This edition published by arrangement with Stewart, Taberi & Chang, New York, New York.

All rights reserved. Except as permitted under the United States Copyright Act of 1976, no part of this publication may be reproduced or distributed in any form or by any means, or stored in a data base or retrieval system, without the prior written permission of the publisher.

SRA Macmillan/McGraw-Hill
250 Old Wilson Bridge Road
Worthington, OH 43085

Printed in the United States of America

ISBN 0-02-685915-7

1 2 3 4 5 6 7 8 9 CDY 99 98 97 96 95 94

arti lived on a small island, in a tiny house, at the base of a very tall tree.

**M**arti was a simple mouse, whose life consisted of simple pleasures: spending time with his best friend Gomez, afternoons in the sun, and a good imported Swiss cheese every now and again.

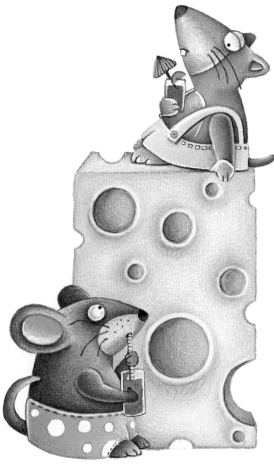

One day, however, Martí was faced with a rather extraordinary task.

He awoke as usual, and, as usual, he did his morning exercises. But when he went outside, he found a note from his friend Gomez tacked to the front of his door.

Dinner Tonight at my house. Bring a mango. — Gomez

"A mango?" thought Martí. "Who ever heard of such a thing? What does a mango look like?" he wondered. "And where on earth can I get one?"

Martí was a very curious mouse.

uickly, Martí put on his lucky shirt and headed out in search of this mysterious mango. First he decided to stop next door at the lily pond, where his neighbor Frog was on his way out.

"Excuse me," said Martí.
"What's a mango?"

"A mango is a fruit!" Frog said, and
—KERPLUNK—disappeared into the pond.

"Now we're getting somewhere," thought Martí. He took out his notebook and made a note that a mango is a fruit, and went on.

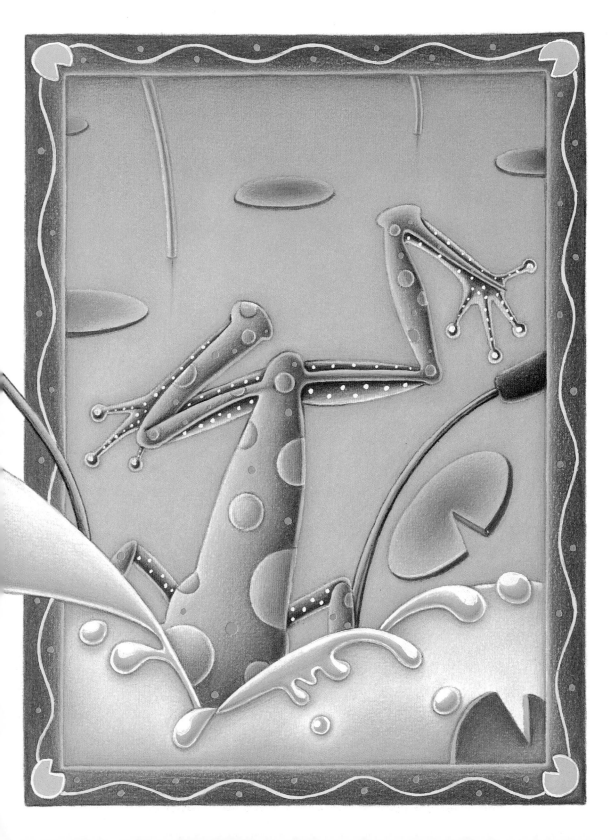

econd, Martí came across a gorilla gathering guavas.

"Excuse me," said Martí, "are those mangos?"

"Of course not," groaned the gorilla. "Mangos are much bigger. These are guavas."

"Thank you," said Martí. He made a note that a mango is a fruit bigger than a guava, and went on.

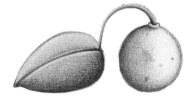

Next, he met a worm working her way through a watermelon.

"Excuse me," said Martí, "is that a mango?"

"Not to my knowledge," whispered the worm. "A mango is much smaller. This is a watermelon."

"Thank you," said Martí. He made a note that a mango is a fruit bigger than a guava, but smaller than a watermelon, and went on.

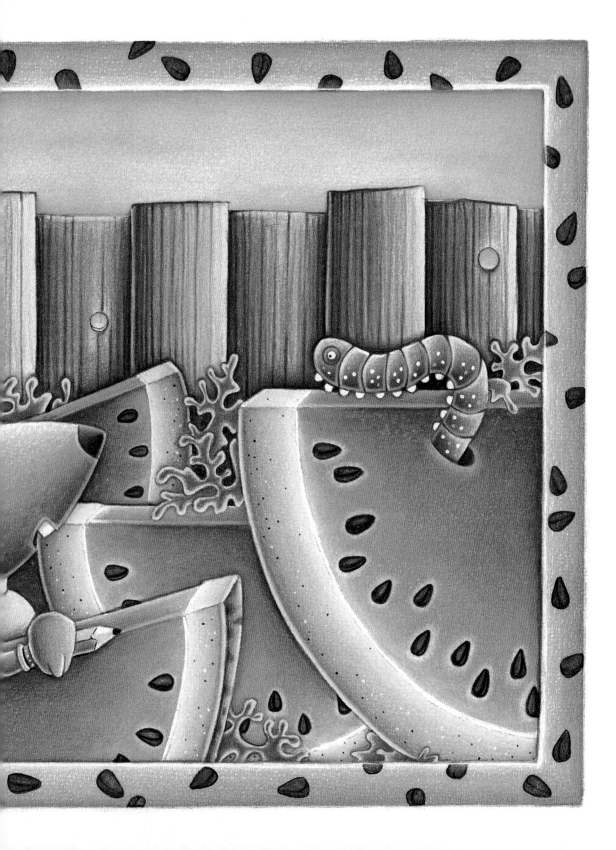

**S**oon after, Martí saw a kangaroo collecting kiwis.

"Excuse me," said Martí, "are those mangos?"

"Not at all," crooned the kangaroo. "Mangos are much smoother. These are kiwis."

"Thank you," said Martí. He made a note that a mango is a fruit bigger than a guava, but smaller than a watermelon, and smoother than a kiwi, and went on.

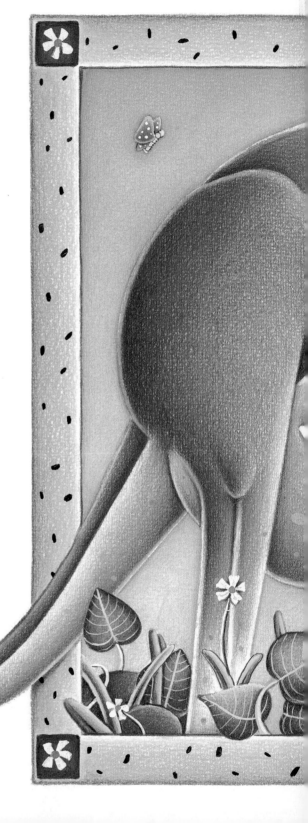

Later, Martí ran into some beavers bearing bananas.

"Excuse me," said Martí, "are those mangos?"

"No, no, no," babbled a beaver. "Mangos are much rounder. These are bananas."

"Thank you," said Martí. He made a note that a mango is a fruit bigger than a guava, but smaller than a watermelon, smoother than a kiwi, and rounder than a banana, and went on.

In the afternoon, Martí came upon a cockroach creeping across a coconut.

"Excuse me," said Martí, "is that a mango?"

"Hardly!" croaked the cockroach. "A mango is much softer. This is a coconut."

"Thank you," said Martí. He made a note that a mango is a fruit bigger than a guava, but smaller than a watermelon, smoother than a kiwi, rounder than a banana, and softer than a coconut, and went on.

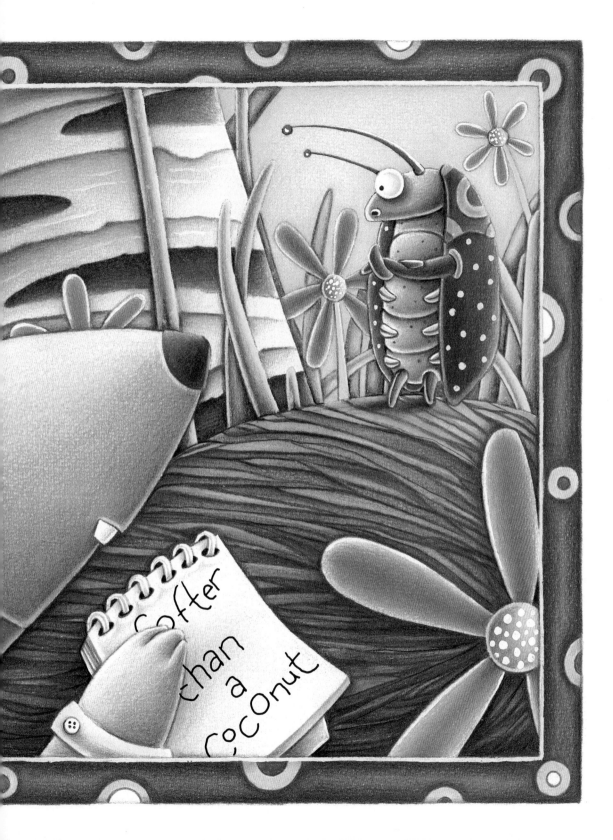

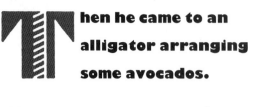 hen he came to an
alligator arranging
some avocados.

"Excuse me," said Martí, "are
those mangos?"

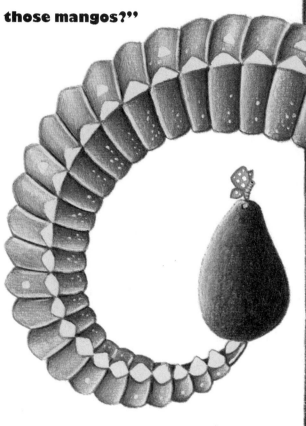

But the alligator did not
answer. So Marti went on.

By now it was getting late, and Martí had become quite discouraged. He decided to head home without his mango. When he got there, he sat down, tired from his search.

"I'll never find this mango," said Martí unhappily. "I can't find anything. I can't go to Gomez's party without a mango. I'm a failure."

Martí was a very depressed mouse.

Just then Frog came bouncing by on a fig.

"I see you've found your mango," he said to Martí.

"Please don't tease me," begged Martí. "I have not found my mango."

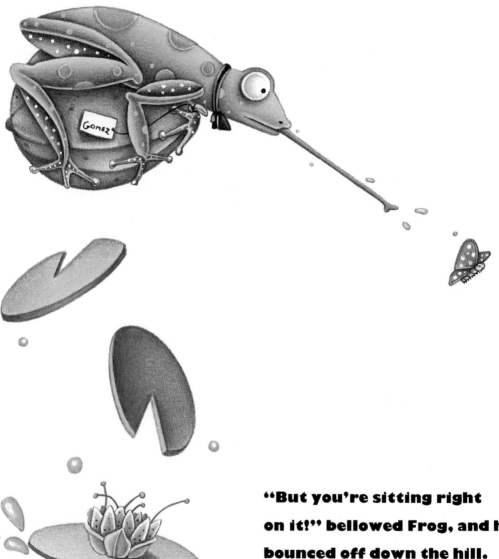

"But you're sitting right on it!" bellowed Frog, and he bounced off down the hill.

Martí looked down to see just what it was he was sitting on. "Could this be a mango?" he thought. He referred to his notes.

a mango is a fruit

Smaller than a Watermelon

Bigger than a guava

Rounder than a Banana

Smoother than a kiwi

Softer than a Coconut

"This *is* a mango!" cheered Martí. And he smiled a very big smile.

Martí was a very happy mouse.

GLOSSARY

Avocado: an American tropical fruit that is pear-shaped and sometimes called an "alligator pear." The green to black skin can be smooth or bumpy, and the inside is a creamy yellow-green.

Banana: an elongated, curved tropical fruit that is green when picked and yellow when ripe.

Coconut: a large hard-shelled seed of the coconut palm tree. The outer shell is hairy and very hard while the inside has white meat and a milky liquid in its hollow center.

Fig: originally from Asia Minor, there are hundreds of varieties of figs, from dark purple ones to ones that are almost white. All have sweet insides with many little edible seeds.

Guava: native to Brazil, guavas can be pear-shaped, oval, or round, and are slightly larger than an egg. The guava's thin skin is first green and then turns pale yellow when ripe. Depending on the variety, the insides of this aromatic fruit can be anything from white to dark pink, and from almost seedless to having many small hard seeds in the center.

Kiwi: a small, almost egg-shaped fruit that is brown and fuzzy on the outside and bright green with tiny black seeds on the inside. Grown in China since ancient times, kiwis are sometimes called "Chinese gooseberries."

Mango: a native of southeast Asia, the mango has been cultivated for over six thousand years. A mango is sometimes called the "apple of the tropics," but is bigger than an apple. The tough skin is green and yellow with a rosy tint, and at the center of the bright orange flesh is a large, hard pit.

Watermelon: a widely cultivated large melon with a green rind; sweet, juicy, red flesh; and shiny black seeds.